gontrand and the CRESCent MOON

Canadian Cataloguing Publication Data

Papineau, Lucie
(Gontrand et le croissant des cavernes. English)
Gontrand and the crescent moon
Translation of: Gontrand et le croissant des cavernes.

ISBN 1-894363-15-9

I. Reno, Alain II. Homel, David III. Title.
IV. Title: Gontrand et le croissant des cavernes. English.

PS8581.A6658G6613 1999   jC843'.54   C99-900526-X
PZ7.P2126Go 1999

Series Editor: Lucie Papineau
Art and Graphic Director: Primeau & Barey

Legal Deposit: 3rd quarter 1999
National Library of Canada
Bibliothèque nationale du Québec

Dominique & Friends
A division of Les éditions Héritage inc.
300 Arran Street, Saint-Lambert, Quebec J4R 1K5
Tel.: (514) 875-0327
Fax: (450) 672-5448
E-mail: info@editionsheritage.com

Printed in Hong Kong
10 9 8 7 6 5 4 3 2

THE CANADA COUNCIL | LE CONSEIL DES ARTS
FOR THE ARTS | DU CANADA
SINCE 1957 | DEPUIS 1957

SODEC
SOCIÉTÉ DE
DÉVELOPPEMENT
DES ENTREPRISES
CULTURELLES
Québec ::

The publisher wishes to thank the Canada Council
for its support, as well as SODEC and Canadian Heritage.

gontrand and the CRESCent MOON

LUCiE PAPiNEAU

ALAiN RENO

English Text: David Homel

Dominique & Friends

A long time ago, so long ago that no one
really remembers, cave men lived on the earth.

They lived in real caves, hunted mammoths and wild buffalos,
and they never combed their hair or washed their ears.

Like all cave children, Gontrand was very happy.
All day long, he played in the forest with his friends,
Doris the laughing dodo bird, Giles the hairy crocodile and Morgan the dragon.

But when darkness fell, covering the world with ink-black night,
Gontrand stopped playing. He would sit in the clearing
and listen to the Masked Sorcerer tell his stories.

"Now comes the realm of the night,"
the Sorcerer said in a voice as deep as a cave.
"Black, impenetrable night, where not a light shines.
At night, the Shadow Giants are king.
They go where they want, they uncoil their long,
crooked fingers among the trees and rocks,
and down every path."

No one ever returned from the Kingdom
of the Shadows.

As the Sorcerer told his tales, Gontrand would snuggle up
with his mother. He loved the way she smelled. She had a smell like croissants that
would melt his fears like butter.

His mother was the queen of a very special tribe:
the Clan of the Pastry Bakers!

Early the next morning, the sun rose and scattered the Giants and their Shadows.
Gontrand and his friends went on a picnic,
and played the greatest game of hide-and-go-seek ever.

On the back of his dodo bird, Gontrand first tried to find Morgan,
his favourite dragon. As usual, that wasn't very hard.
She had slipped behind a daisy that was really much too small.

The three friends went off in search of Giles.
There was no crocodile in the giant frogs' nest,
nor under the fronds of the pink coconut trees,
and no one was hiding in the den of the three-eyed moles.

There was neither hide nor hair
of Giles the hairy crocodile!

From flower to flower, from hiding place to
hiding place, Gontrand and his friends
moved deeper into the heart of the forest.
"Olly, olly ocean free, Giles!" they called.
"We give up, you win.
Where are you, anyway?"

But there was no answer.
　　"Hurry up, we have to get back to the clearing before dark!"
Not even a whisper of an answer.

　　"He must be in the lily pad river," Doris the dodo bird whispered.
　　"Come on, we'll sneak up on him!"

There was Giles the crocodile, snoring away
in the middle of the stinky lily pads.
"We found you!" Gontrand shouted,
and he jumped into the river.
"We win!" Morgan declared, splashing him with water.
"Wake up," Doris said, pulling on his tail.
"What's going on?"
asked Giles in a voice thick with sleep.

"Good night, everyone!" the sun called out, then lay down
below the horizon.
The four friends looked at one another. They were worried.

Night had crept up on them, and there they were
in the heart of the deep forest, far from the clearing.

They shivered together with cold and fear.
Gontrand's heart beat like a drum: boom-boom, boom-boom.
The wind whipped the branches of the ghostly trees,
screech-screech, screech-screech, like a violin out of tune.

Gontrand closed his eyes. He was too afraid to watch the dance of the
Shadow Giants: boom-screech-boom, their long, crooked limbs jiggling.
Soon, he knew, the giants would be here.
Their twisted fingers were already creeping among
the rocks and trees, and moving down the path.
Darkness was their kingdom.

Meanwhile, in the clearing,
                what was Gontrand's mother, the Queen of Pastry, doing?
                She was baking croissants, what else?
        She was working so hard she didn't notice that night was falling.

When at last she lifted her eyes from her golden dough,
                she saw that evening had slipped into night.
        "Gontrand," she whispered, "where's my Gontrand gone to?"
                Only the rustling of shadows between the trees answered her.

        The Queen of Pastry felt her heart grow cold.
        A tiny voice – could it be Gontrand's? – echoed in her ears:
        No one has ever returned from the Kingdom of the Shadows – no one!

        "No!" she cried out against the night.
                        "You'll come back, I swear!"

Suddenly, dark black smoke
began to sting her eyes.
        "My croissants!" she realized. "They're burning."
        The Queen of Pastry ran to her oven.
The fire was dancing, hot and red.
The smoke escaped and went swirling skyward
with the wind. Looking up with stinging eyes,
        the Queen of Pastry gasped with surprise.

A sliver of light had flown out of the oven along with the smoke.
The light of a golden crescent. Carried upward by the heat of the oven,
it shone very high in the sky, illuminating the night.

The Queen of Pastry looked up in wonder.
Her wish had been granted, in the form of a great glowing crescent.

Deep in the forest, a warm breeze came and brushed Gontrand's cheek.

"Mama? Is that you?"

He opened one eye, then the other.

He discovered the marvelous crescent of light.

The shadows pulled back between the trees, revealing the lost path.

The Shadow Giants fell silent.

"I can see!" Gontrand cried. "I can see in the night."

Quickly, very quickly, the boy, the dodo bird, the crocodile

and the young dragon ran down the path,

guided by the golden light.

Gontrand was the first cave child
who could find his way in the dark.
The Masked Sorcerer threw a party that lasted all week.

Ever since then, the Queen of Pastry heats up her oven only once night has fallen.
In the sky, sometimes the light is as round as a pumpernickel.
Sometimes it looks like half a cream pie.
Other times it's exactly like a plump, buttery, golden croissant.

Gontrand was the first one to name the light. He called it **Moon**.

Which is why, when evening falls, we can see the moon shining with its many faces.
To help us find our way in the night.
To make people who are cold feel warmer.
And to make the Shadow Giants disappear.

Because the great-great-great-great-great granddaughter
of the Queen of Pastry still makes
the best croissants in the whole world!